# The Serpent and the Sun

# The Serpent and the Sun

*Myths of the Mexican World*

Retold, and with decorations, by Cal Roy

Farrar, Straus and Giroux : New York

TO MY MOTHER AND FATHER

# Contents

# The Serpent and the Sun

*The sun eagle devouring a human heart.*
*From a Toltec carving*

# Foreword

Atop the tallest pyramid in Tenochtitlan, capital of the Aztec nation, two temples shared one lofty platform —the blue and white temple of the rain god Tlaloc, and the red and white temple of Huitzilopochtli, god of the sun and war. The view from that dizzying height embraced two volcanoes and five lakes, causeways that tied the island city to the mainland, palaces, floating gardens, an arcaded marketplace, and the emperor's private park and zoo. Around the twin temples ran a serpent-headed wall enclosing the great ceremonial center of Tenochtitlan—slaughterhouse of the gods.

Sun worship was the official religion of the Aztec state. But it was not a kindly sun to which black-painted priests sent prayers and offerings; it was the blazing emblem of an empire never at peace, an empire with an incredible mission—to keep the sun alive by sacrificing prisoners of war. Holding equal sway over the people, and tempering the official religion, however, was the old religion of the life-giving, wisdom-dispensing rain god.

The Aztecs founded their lake-bound capital in 1370 and began empire-building in 1430. Eight hundred years earlier, in a valley thirty miles away, the civilization of Teotihuacan had reached its peak, extending its influence as far south as Guatemala and as far into history as the Aztec empire. Teotihuacan had been an unfortified city ruled by priests who, as far as we know, kept peace throughout a vast domain for more than five centuries. Most of the gods later worshipped by the Aztecs were worshipped at Teotihuacan with little or no human sacrifice on their altars.

*The rain god, as pictured on a vase*
*from Teotihuacan*

These gentler gods were headed by the great god of rain.

But a change in religious beliefs and practices swept central Mexico with invading hunting tribes from the north. Teotihuacan fell—no one knows how—and was abandoned—no one knows why. Much of its knowledge in the arts, science, and religion became the heritage of Tulsa, a new city founded by a people of unknown origin—perhaps descendants of the conquerors of Teotihuacan. The Toltecs of Tula, too, were ruled by priest-kings, but these peaceful rulers were driven out at last by warrior-kings. Then, after Tula's mysterious collapse, the Toltecs settled in the valley of the five lakes, and new hordes of barbarians appeared. Among these newcomers were the Aztecs. Vassals of the Toltecs at first, they eventually became their conquerors. As a growing military nation, the Aztecs independently developed their religion of war based on the endless feeding of the sun on human hearts, but the old religion of the rain god was part of their inheritance and steadfastly survived—though it, too, became drenched with blood.

Out of the rain god's worship had grown a symbol that lent itself to all times and all peoples in ancient Mexico—the symbol of the Plumed Serpent. In Teotihuacan it represented the waters of the earth and probably the earth itself, covered with plume-like vegetation. In Tula, the Plumed Serpent became a sky symbol and the name chosen by ruling priests. The Aztecs awarded Plumed Serpent a place in the heavens as god of the wind and morning star. He presided over their school of priests, astrologers, and statesmen, while his traditional enemy, Smoking Mirror, was patron of the school of warriors. To the Maya of Yucatan, Plumed Serpent was the Toltec intruders' sign of conquest, and to the Maya of the southern Mexican and Guatemalan highlands, he was a water god who created order out of chaos and gave men life.

These two religions—one dedicated to war and the

*The Plumed Serpent. From an Aztec carving*

other to life and learning—illustrate the main idea underlying Aztec mythology: all things are made up of two opposing forces. The Aztecs believed that the world was created through the combined efforts of two gods usually at war with one another, and that the first man was formed from bones stolen from the underworld and blood freely given by the gods. But the best illustration of this duality is the Plumed Serpent itself. It unites in its image sky and earth, spirit and matter, representing the energy flowing between this world and heaven when man cooperates with those who rule his destiny. As we shall see, the myths of ancient Mexico as well as those of the inheritors, the Mexican Indians of today, are tales of violence, yet all of them contain seeds of a profound spiritual philosophy. Perhaps the rain god's blue and white temple sharing equal space with the red and white temple of the war god stood for the double nature of man himself.

In 1521, Tenochtitlan fell to Spaniards led by Hernando Cortés. The victors razed the Aztec metropolis and drained the five lakes to build a new capital—Mexico City. In their determined destruction of everything they regarded as pagan, the picture books recording Aztec religious beliefs were burned. In all Mexico only seventeen—painted in colors on bark paper and opening out, page after page, in accordion folds—survived the bonfires. These, together with the manuscripts of books written immediately after the conquest by Indians and their new missionary teachers, are the codices—ancient historical records—from which many of the illustrations in this book have been redrawn. Each codex is named after its discoverer, its sometime owner, or the place where it can now be found.

Among the most industrious of the missionary teachers who collected information on the culture destroyed by overzealous conquerors was a Franciscan friar named Bernardino de Sahagún. The encyclopedic notes he gathered into his *General History of the Things of New Spain,* along with the *History of the Indies of New Spain* by the Dominican friar Diego Durán, are two of the best sources we have for studying the mythology of ancient central Mexico. Two works by Christianized Aztecs—the *History of the Chichimecas* by Alva Ixtlixochitl and the *Mexican Chronicle* by Alvarado Tezozomoc—as well as the *History of the Mexicans According to Their Paintings,* the *Legend of the Suns,* and the *Annals of Cuauhtitlan* by unknown authors add to our knowledge of Aztec beliefs. These are the sources from which most of the myths in this book have been written.

But the Aztecs were not the only or even the greatest nation in Mexico before the Spanish conquest. Among the many peoples inhabiting middle America in the sixteenth century, the Maya of southeastern Mexico and Guatemala represented an even higher civilization than that of Tenochtitlan. By 1521, the once vast Mayan nation had broken up into many small nations, but they preserved the wisdom of their ancestors in codices written in hieroglyphics. Unfortunately, only three Mayan codices escaped destruction by fire and their hieroglyphic writing is still a puzzle to modern scholars. So our richest source for Mayan myths is the *Popol Vuh*, the *Book of the Council* of the Quiché Maya who emigrated from Mexico to Guatemala. It was written in the Mayan tongue by an unknown Indian tutored by Spanish missionaries.

The myths of ancient Mexico tell of beginnings. They take place in a sacred time that is not like our time, and one must not try to understand them as one understands history. They ignore all limits that we would place upon a story to make it believable. So we shall find that immortal gods can die, yet do not die for all time. The moon may be a god or a goddess. The gods, in fact, take on any form that may be convenient for them (or meaningful to the myth) and are represented in art either as human figures, animals, or combinations of the two.

Just as the myths treat of beginnings, they also set patterns of destiny. The gods allow themselves to be sacrificed to demonstrate to the Aztec people how they must sacrifice themselves. The myth of Hummingbird's people tells about a nation with a prophecy and a promised land. The myth of the twins from the *Popol Vuh* recounts the destiny of all good and wise men—death and resurrection.

The people who produced these myths have not disappeared in Mexico. Among the many Indian groups who still inhabit the country, the old traditions are preserved, and myths missing in ancient documents are frequently found in the stories, songs, and prayers of present-day Indians such as the Huichols of Nayarit and Jalisco and the Mixe of the mountains of Oaxaca. These modern keepers of an ancient light of wisdom are the inheritors of the Axtecs and Maya of pre-conquest Mexico.

# AZTEC MYTHS

*The earth monster. From an Aztec carving*

# The Monster We Live On

Before there was anything else, there was darkness—darkness and the hollow roar of the sea stretching from nowhere to nowhere. There was no land to be called by any name.

The only living thing in the black sea was a monster. She was there before anything else. Only the gods and the sea itself were older than she was. Some say she was a giant shark or a crocodile almost as big as the ocean she swam in or a mountainous toad. She had thousands of eyes and noses and mouths.

In the dark heavens above the sea lived two gods with a single thought, to create the earth and man. One of the gods was called Plumed Serpent. His splendor shone in the heavens like chiseled sparks of water-green jade. On his head he wore a tall hat trimmed with ocelot fur and flowing feathers of red, green, and gold. The feathers made a faint sound, as of future birds singing. The earrings of the god were fiery turquoise and around his throat lay a golden collar hung with many seashells. His sandals were white, trimmed with pearls. About his legs were tied many bells. On one arm Plumed Serpent carried a shield adorned with a sign called the wind jewel, and over his face he wore a mask that looked like the beak of a large bird. This was the wind mask, for Plumed Serpent was the morning star who swept the road to the gates of dawn.

The second god was black as night, but he had a band of yellow painted across his eyes and another across his mouth. Young and handsome, he wore gold earrings, black sandals, and rattlesnake rattles on his legs. The hair on one side of his head hung down. On

*Plumed Serpent's wind mask, as shown in the Codex Borgia*

the other side it was combed upward. Future warriors would wear their hair this way in his honor. But this god was more than a warrior; he was a sorcerer too. He could change himself into a jaguar, a star, a human skeleton, a turkey. He could drop from the sky by a spider's thread. He could make himself invisible. About him floated an icy air. Was it the chill of northern ice and snow in the region of the heavens from which he came, or was it the shivering breath of eerie things, of death and witchcraft? White heron feathers floated from his rattling headdress.

Donning his wind mask, Plumed Serpent blew upon the dark waters below. The waters separated and showed the gods where the sea monster lay. Together they descended from one heaven to another until they had passed through nine in all. But before they

reached the water they turned themselves into serpents.

Then, working together, they attacked.

Mountains of foam spiraled from the churning waters. Torrents poured down as the tail of the infuriated
monster flung wave after wave aloft. Between them,
god and god locked her in gigantic, crushing coils,
squeezing her, stretching her, and finally parting her
in two. The struggle lasted longer than any struggle
since. But in the end the monster was divided.

Her upper half sank to the bottom of the sea, the
highest points of her craggy surface rising out of the
waves to become what we call land. Shored continents,
cliff-skirted peninsulas, and islands ringed with ruf-
fled beaches were formed. The heavens felt something
new pressing up from below—mountains, hills, and
plains. The monster had been converted into earth.

Not yet finished with their task, Plumed Serpent
and the other god stood on the land risen from the sea
to raise the monster's lower half. One at one end of
the world and one at the other, they planted themselves like trees and slowly raised their arms. Sea
water poured through their fingers and down their

*Hieroglyphic sign meaning Smoking Mirror*

sides as they pushed up the underside of the monster higher than the mountain tops. They hung it in space above the stars, to become the distant, all-encircling sky.

Meanwhile, the monster's sunken half was still changing its appearance. From her hair sprouted grass, from her scaly skin flowers of many colors. From her thousands of eyes gushed inland seas, lakes, rivers, springs. Some flowed clear, reflecting the stars. Others lay in murky pools. Her mouths hardened to form deep caves. And her noses froze into the rocks of tall mountains.

This is how the gods created the earth. But one of the gods paid for the harm done to the sea monster.

During the fight, Plumed Serpent's partner lost one foot. The hot blood smoked as it poured from the wound. It glittered like glass. He could see his face reflected in it—his face, which is the night-sky itself. That one-footed god is called Smoking Mirror.

*The sunken sun, the sun of night.*
*Redrawn from the Codex Borgia*

# The Fifth Sun

Darkness above and darkness below, and in the dark was a stillness awaiting the unfolding of light—so was the world, like a sleeper on the verge of a dream. The nine-storied heavens were silent; the third heaven, called the House of the Sun, was still an empty corridor. The gates of dawn remained closed and the stars gave but a faint glow to the newly formed earth.

One by one the great gods took their place above

the clouds to create a sun. But the first sun collapsed under a soggy sky, the second was destroyed by jaguars, the third by a rain of fire, and the fourth by hurricanes. None of them moved across the sky and none was able to give enduring light and life to the earth.

When it came time to create a fifth sun, all the gods met in a valley between wooded hills, at a place called Teotihuacan, Where the Gods Are Born. There was nothing there then, neither temples nor pyramids. Only darkness.

First one god, then another spoke to the gathering. "Let us be friends here," they said. "It is time to know our faces." But though they spoke with "flowers on their lips" as it is said, all their fine speeches led up to only one question—who would sacrifice himself to become the fifth sun? For it was plain that in order to create a lasting sun a great sacrifice was necessary. Only by giving his life could some god conquer night.

The only god who responded to this question was one named Shell of the Sea. He was a proud god, though not an important one. Pride, rather than love or courage, made him speak out, to offer himself as the victim. Through his foolish head danced visions of ruling the heavens and receiving honors from the altars of men.

But the gods were not satisfied with only one volunteer, one victim. Perhaps the disaster which had doomed sun after sun made them think that two might succeed where one had failed four times before.

"Who else?" they asked. But there was no other Shell of the Sea. No one came forward to offer himself. One god looked at another, then quickly away, none of them willing to lose his life.

Silence fell. Fear bred hostility. Then somehow all the gods happened to look in the same direction at the same time and their eyes lit upon a sickly member of their group known as the Scabby One. Some say he was Plumed Serpent's son and that he had no mother. The same thought occurred to all—here was their scapegoat.

"Let you be the one who lights the world," the gods said to him. Their voices rang with the encouragement cowards offer the weak.

"So be it," the Scabby One replied. "I will do whatever you tell me."

The two victims chosen, two mountains were built. Earth was heaped up, Stones set one against the other to form steps and platforms, and thus the pyramids were built at Teotihuacan. Then Shell of the Sea went up to the top of one pyramid and the Scabby One went up the other to make offerings and do penance before the great sacrifice.

An enormous fire was built and fed for four days, during which Shell of the Sea and the Scabby One prepared themselves for the ordeal. Shell of the Sea made splendid offerings on his altar. Instead of pine boughs he offered precious quetzal plumes. Instead of balls of dried grass he offered little balls of gold. And in place of thorns from the maguey he gave thorns of jade. Those thorns that should have been stained with his own blood he replaced with thorns made of red coral. The incense he burned was the finest he could buy.

The Scabby One, on the other hand, was too poor to make such fine offerings. Instead of pine boughs he offered common rushes. Along with maguey thorns wrapped in balls of dried grass he offered many thorns reddened with the blood of his ears, arms, and thighs. For incense he burned the scabs that covered his body.

When the four days had passed and the fire blazed like the heart of a volcano, Shell of the Sea came down from his pyramid magnificently dressed in white plumes. The Scabby One appeared wearing ornaments of bark paper. Both victims stood at one end of an avenue formed by two straight lines of gods facing one another. At the other end the flames extended themselves like a butterfly unfolding its wings.

"You, Shell of the Sea, enter the fire!" one of the gods boomed out.

Feeling all eyes upon him, Shell of the Sea sprinted forward. But when the great heat of the fire kissed his cheeks and bit his forehead, he wheeled like an animal that takes fright in the midst of charging.

Recovering himself, he leaped in the direction of the fire once more. But again his courage failed him and he turned aside and stumbled backward. Four times he tried to hurl himself into the flames and four times he quailed at the heat. Four times were all he was allowed to try.

Then the spokesmen for the gods roared out, "You, Scabby One, enter the fire!"

And like a bird dropping on its prey, the sickly god raced forward and seized the flames, sputtering as he fell in their midst.

Then what Shell of the Sea lacked in courage was

*The Scabby One burning, as shown in the Codex Borgia*

made up for in shame. Flying into the circle of heat, he too cast himself into the fire. Down from the dark sky hurtled a white eagle to rise out of the flames burned brown. An ocelot ran quickly through the fire, scorching itself only in spots. The hawk and the coyote also toasted themselves in the fire of sacrifice.

By then the darkness was turning from black to red. The gods scanned the sky to see in what direction dawn would appear, and in the east two red disks mounted the hills.

"What is this?" asked the gods upon seeing the double sunrise. The rays of one sun overlapped the other's, both being of equal strength. "They will blind us when they reach the zenith together," they said. "If there must be two suns in the sky, one should give less light than the other."

So one of the gods caught a rabbit by the ears and, running, hurled it toward the eastern horizon. The rabbit struck the face of the disk formed from the glowing spirit of Shell of the Sea, dimming its light and creating the moon; and there the rabbit may be seen to this day. But some say that the light of the sun and the light of the moon were unequal from the beginning. According to them, Shell of the Sea did not reach the flames when he threw himself into the fire. Dying in the ashes, he rose ash-white into the sky.

But the sun, he who had been the Scabby One, hung red and feverish above the eastern hills, too weak to climb the blue stairway of the gods. Its rays struck the earth like arrows of flame.

"What will we do?" the gods wondered. "We can't live like this."

But for four days the exhausted sun rested without moving. Then a hawk was sent to ask the reason for its weakness, and the messenger returned saying that the sun could not move without first drinking the blood of the gods.

Angered at such a demand, the god of twilight cried

*The rabbit on the moon. Redrawn from the Codex Borgia*

out, "Why don't I shoot him down then, this feeble good-for-nothing sun?"

But the god's dark arrows only streaked the sky and could not entirely extinguish the sun's glow.

Then, rather than fail the sun they had created with such effort, all the gods consented to die. The wind god was their executioner. And when they had all fallen by his arrows and the sun had fed on their hearts, the wind blew strongly against the sun until it was well on its way upward. Later, he puffed at the pale moon, who followed a little behind the sun. But the moon was further held up at a crossroads by elves and demons who wished to preserve a period of darkness. Thus they divided night from day.

This fifth sun, our sun, is called the sun of movement. Some day, we are told, it will be destroyed by earthquakes.

*The flower symbol of Xochiquetzal.*
*Redrawn from the Codex Borgia*

# Hermit into Scorpion

Three sisters, fairest of all the goddesses, met in the sky above a desert. One was Lady of the Skirt of Stars, whose powdery garment is flung like a veil across the night sky, making a starry path for the gods.

The second of the goddesses was Lady of the Skirt of Jade. Her head was bound with blue ribbons edged with pearls. The curling hem of her skirt sparkled with jewels like whitecaps studding the edge of the sea, tumbling on sunny beaches, and dispersing in foam. She was the goddess of rivers, lakes, and seas.

The third sister, Xochiquetzal, whose name means Plumed or Precious Flower, was the most beautiful of the three. She was the laughter-filled goddess of love. At times she was forced to leave her home, a rose-covered mountain of funny dwarfs and sunny musicians and boys and girls whose dancing made you wonder if they were birds or butterflies, for a land of turquoise mists and showers in the rain god's realm. There she was hidden in a cave and the same game was played each year—the young sun, the Boy Prince, went looking for her. From this game of love the corn was born anew. At other times Precious Flower could often be found in the jewel market. Jade earrings and nose ornaments delighted her. And wherever she went she adorned herself with garlands of flowers while two flashing plumes of the quetzal bird floated from her scented hair.

Now when the three sisters met, one spoke, pointing to the wilderness below where a gaunt and sunburned hermit sat on a pinnacle of rock called Drum of Stone.

"That is Yaupan," said the goddess. "He has left

his arrows, his shield, his lance, his wife, and his children. He who was a warrior and head of a family has come here to the desert to fast and pray, to strengthen himself by self-denial and suffering. He knows that soon the gods intend to change him into a scorpion, the first of that race. As part of his saintly preparation, he has vowed never to speak to women. But look, sisters, if Yaupan becomes so strong through acts of penance, what will he be when he becomes a scorpion? His poison will be so powerful men will die of his sting without hope or remedy. One of us should tempt him and thus weaken the poison of all his breed. Then men may hope to survive his sting."

The other goddesses agreed with their sister's words. And who but the fairest of the three was best qualified to speak to the saint, to make him speak to her and break his vow?

Then Precious Flower descended through the burning air and dust-dark whirlwinds to earth, becoming visible at the base of the rock on which Yaupan sat. The earth was like fire beneath her feet and the rock was like a needle, nearly impossible to scale.

"Yaupan," called the goddess softly from below his perch. "Yaupan."

*Olmec figure in meditation*

Her voice was low the many times she called him. "Yaupan."

Though his ears were turned away from sounds that reminded him of his wife and other women, Precious Flower never raised her voice. It was but a raindrop falling in that arid silence. Its sound tinkled and reflected and formed a shimmering butterfly before the hermit's eyes. And when he paid heed at last, she spoke to him even more softly than before.

"Yaupan," she pleaded, "look at me. I am at your feet and helpless."

And Yaupan looked.

The eyes of the goddess were his ruin. He saw every color of the heavens in them.

"Yaupan," she wept, her face shining like a jewel, "help me up to where you are."

And Yaupan went down and helped her up.

"Speak to me," she begged him when they were together atop the Drum of Stone.

And Yaupan spoke. Forgetting his vow, forgetting he had abandoned the world to strengthen himself, Yaupan softened under the goddess's gaze.

But the two of them, goddess and saint, were not alone in the desert. An enemy hid in the shadows, spying. Some say it was Smoking Mirror, sent by the gods to watch him who was to become a scorpion. Seeing the goddess and hermit together, the enemy sprang forth to accuse Yaupan of breaking his hermit's vow.

The goddess vanished. The triumphant enemy mounted the rock and with a single stroke cut off the hermit's head. Arms upraised to defend himself, Yaupan was hurled to the rocks below. His transformation from man to scorpion was instantaneous. And under the rocks he made his home, armed with poison that is often deadly but not always so.

But the gods who had sent the enemy to spy on Yaupan had not given him leave to kill. To punish

*A scorpion. From the Codex Borgia*

him for his angry act, they turned him into a lobster, forcing him to walk with claws upraised, as though carrying something before him—something, if you could see it, resembling Yaupan's severed head.

*The wind god. From a sculpture
from Tenochtitlan*

# The Wind's Bride

In the heat of afternoon, the young goddess Mayahuel lay sleeping with others of her own age, guarded by a chaperone as ugly as she was ancient. Ugly of temper, ugly of face and of form, the guardian goddess dozed off only to wake up again, run her eyes over the girls in her charge, and nod back to sleep. All the girls were lovely, all on the verge of womanhood, and Mayahuel was both the loveliest and the closest to that change which comes about when the heart flowers.

As the old chaperone's chin dropped once more to her breastbone, a breeze stole through the open window, touching Mayahuel's cheek and whispering in her ear. At first it spoke of dreadful things, of a visit to the land of the dead that lies beneath the earth. It told her how Plumed Serpent, like the sun when it drops in the west, had made that journey to rob the lords of the dead of certain precious bones. Fleeing to earth with them, he asked Serpent Woman to grind them like corn. Then, when the ground bones had been sprinkled with blood drawn from the bodies of the gods, he molded the dough-like substance into the shapes of a young man and a young woman. These were the first people on earth, the breeze whispered to Mayahuel.

Then it sang two joyous songs. One told how Plumed Serpent deceived the ants and stole corn from the Mountain of Sustenance for man's food. The other told how he, wearing his wind mask, had flown to the House of the Sun and there, on the stairways of light, kidnapped the musicians of the sun so that man might enjoy music, that he might sing and dance.

But still there was something missing in man's life, the breeze went on to say. As yet, men and women did not know love.

And then the breeze told Mayahuel that she and he, Plumed Serpent, might teach man what only the gods had known till then.

Listening, dreaming, waking, sighing, Mayahuel at last smiled her consent. Putting her arm about Plumed Serpent's neck, she let him carry her out through the window and down to earth.

When the ancient chaperone woke up and once more ran her eyes over the girls she guarded as though they were made of fine gold, she saw to her horror that one was missing.

"Mayahuel!" she called. "Mayahuel!"

But when there was no answer after calling twice, she screamed until the heavens echoed, not with the name of the little goddess but with that of the she-devils who were at the ancient one's beck. A nest of poisonous spiders could not be more terrifying than the swarm of demons who gathered quickly about her. A word from the ancient chaperone to inform them of Mayahuel's disappearance, and they dropped to earth in pursuit.

*The first man and woman, as pictured in the Codex Borgia*

The earth trembled beneath their furious search. Sawing with their mouths, trampling with their legs, they swept through fields and forests, leaving havoc and waste behind, as though a rain of meteors had pitted the earth, ripped branches from trees, and left corn lying broken on its stalk. They searched until they found a tree of such splendid proportions they knew it could not have sprung from seed but from the very bodies of Plumed Serpent and his stolen bride. The thick-boled tree spread wide in two flowering branches, and in one branch the thwarted chaperone recognized her missing charge.

No sooner did the ancient goddess call out her discovery than the tree split, both branches falling to the ground. The goddess and her spider-demons pounced upon the branch into which the body of Mayahuel had been transformed and tore it to pieces with claws and teeth, scattering fragments wildly about the earth and casting others up to the sky.

When the insane swarm, their rage spent, returned to their home among the stars, Plumed Serpent took on his godly form once more and wept as he looked upon the sad destruction of his bride. With painstaking care he searched for fragments of the unfortunate young goddess and lovingly buried them. In time a plant with pointed leaves sprang up in every place that a bit of Mayahuel's body had been hidden. Men called the plant maguey, used its wind-kissed leaves for paper, its spines for needles, its fibers for thread, and discovered at its heart the sweet honey-water from which they learned to make the wine called pulque. Then, in the warmth and glow with which the wine filled them, in the feeling of oneness with each other and with God, men found love.

*The moon with bells tattooed on her cheeks.*
*From an Aztec sculpture*

# Hummingbird of the South

All in white from her eagle-down headdress to her
snakeskin sandals, Lady of the Skirt of Serpents was
sweeping the area before the temple on Serpent Mountain when she saw a tiny ball of hummingbird feathers dancing about her feet in the dust. Picking them
up, she admired the patterns of iridescent colors in
the plumes and tucked them away into her skirt for
safekeeping. They felt warm, as though they had
come from the sun.

Later, Lady of the Skirt of Serpents missed the ball of feathers. Look where she might, it was nowhere to be found. But not long afterward she realized that she was to become a mother.

It would not be for the first time. The child to come already had a grown sister, the moon, a great, temperamental girl whose cheeks were strangely tattooed with golden bells. And there were four hundred brothers as well, four hundred stars who were now grown warriors. Some say the Lady of the Skirt of Serpents was Plumed Serpent's mother too, that he was born after she swallowed a piece of jade. But others say she was only his nurse and that his real mother died in the cave where he was born.

Be that as it may, four hundred and one in the family were enough to make trouble. The sister started it, and before the new child was born, one of the four hundred brothers came to warn Lady of the Skirt of Serpents that she might be killed by her jealous children.

"Don't be frightened, Mother," the voice of the child within her advised when the earth goddess received this news. "I know what I have to do."

So Lady of the Skirt of Serpents put her fears to one side.

Some time later, however, the same brother re-turned to warn that the danger was not only real but near at hand.

"They're on the march," he said, "led by my sister, the moon. They're dressed for war and armed with barbed arrows, and my sister has given them paper banners and drilled them like a squadron."

Again the unborn child spoke. "Watch," he told his older brother, "and tell me how they advance. Where are they now?"

Climbing up to the highest peak of Serpent Moun-tain, the older brother kept the child and his mother informed of the army's movements. As it came closer, the child made ready. And just as the three hundred and ninety-nine led by their sister began to scale the sides of the mountain, he was born fully armed, springing forth like an eager young warrior. On his tiny arm he carried a shield of eagle feathers as bright as the sun and in one plump hand he impatiently balanced a turquoise dart thrower and darts of blue. Fine glossy feathers floated from his headdress and his left leg was covered with hummingbird feathers. Yellow stripes streaked his face while his arms and thighs were painted the color of the noonday sky.

*The Fire Serpent. From an Aztec carving*

No sooner was he born than he commanded his brother to ignite his dart thrower, called Fire Serpent. The first of his flaming darts struck down the leader of the rebellious band. Then leaping toward the others, he made the bells tied to their ankles rattle as they turned and fled. Four times he chased them like rabbits around Serpent Mountain, cutting down one after another with his darts. Many died in flight. Others stopped and begged for mercy but the little warrior had none to show. They did not live long enough to clash shields again. Only a few of those who took to their heels reached the southern horizon safely.

Then the child went about, stripping the fallen and collecting the scattered arms of the defeated. Making

*A hummingbird sucking flowers
on the headdress of a dead warrior.
Redrawn from the Codex Borgia*

a huge pile of battle trophies, he shouted jubilantly—

> *I am Huitzilopochtli, the young warrior,*
> *Hummingbird of the South.*
> *Not in vain do I wear yellow feathers,*
> *For it is I who make the sun rise!*
> *There, at the wall of the region that burns,*
> *Plumes appear. The war cry is heard!*
> *I am called Defender of Men.*

Hummingbird of the South was indeed a defender,
and a tireless leader in the never-ending battle with
night. The souls of warriors who died fighting on
earth and the souls of prisoners who died on the altar

of sacrifice went to the sky to fight at his side. After four years of service they were turned into humming-birds and released to drink flowers in the House of the Sun. But the god who is always as young as the dawn leaps daily to the slaughter of the stars, killing the forces of night to make way for day.

*Plumed Serpent column from Chichen-Itzá,*
*a Mayan city conquered by the Toltecs*

# Plumed Serpent in Tula

Unequaled on earth were the serpent-pillared palaces of Tula, one more marvelous than another. There were rooms with walls as gold as the sun, silver as the moon, turquoise and emerald as the sea, pearl-colored as the dawn. Vast halls and chambers were encrusted with seashells or tapestried with birds' feathers. A sparkling bathing palace spanned the river and underground treasure rooms overflowed with jewels, carved jade, and wrought silver and gold.

But the walls of the room where Quetzalcoatl, Plumed Serpent, lived were bare as the walls of a cave. Though he reigned in Tula, and his reign produced abundance, he spent his days in shadow and his nights in utter darkness, fasting, meditating, and performing acts of penance that left him ill for loss of blood. Pages stood outside his door barring entrance to all lest they disturb the king-priest at his devotions.

At the age of nine, Plumed Serpent had avenged the death of his father, the great hunter Cloud Serpent, by slaying his murderers and erecting a temple over his grave. At the age of twenty-seven, he built a house with green crossbeams in Tulancingo, where he did penance for four years. Then the lords and people of Tulsa asked him to rule over them, for there was no one as wise as he. The god Plumed Serpent worshipped was he who dwells in the innermost heaven, known both as She of the Starry Skirt and as He Who Created the World, Lord and Lady of our Flesh. shipped was he who dwells in the innermost heaven, where opposites are harmoniously united—to the Lord of the Near and the Far he directed his prayers.

*A man carrying a giant cacao pod.*
*From an Aztec sculpture*

The wisdom and saintliness of their ruler was reflected in the peace and plenty enjoyed by the Toltecs.
Although they were said to be taller and longer-
limbed than ordinary men, the squash that grew on
their vines were so big around that a man could not
take one up in his arms and hope to touch the fingers
of one hand with the other. Ears of corn were so huge
that only one could be carried at a time. Cotton grew
in many colors—red, yellow, dark gold, pink, purple,
green, blue-green, deep blue, and orange. In flowering cacao trees roosted birds of every species, their
plumage bright as polished stones and gay as wild
flowers.

Science and the arts also flourished under Plumed

Serpent's guidance. The wise Toltecs discovered the long calendar called the Count of the Year and the short calendar called the Count of Days and Destinies. They could predict lucky and unlucky days, knowing how the heavens move and the names of all the stars. Their work with feathers and jewels has never been surpassed. And this pursuit of knowledge and beauty, along with their enjoyment of the fruits of the earth, followed the paths of peace. Plumed Serpent taught his people to love one another and human blood was no longer shed on the altars of sacrifice. But at the same time the jealous nature of a warrior god was roused. Tezcatlipoca, Smoking Mirror, set his heart on ruling Tula in Plumed Serpent's place.

One day a young man dressed in the rich robes of a magician appeared at the door of Plumed Serpent's cell. No one recognized him. Certainly no one suspected he could be a god. He carried something that was wrapped up in many finely embroidered pieces of cloth.

"Tell our lord Plumed Serpent that I would show him his image," said the sorcerer to the pages on guard. His voice was commanding, his eyes as black and threatening as obsidian knives. But the page who went to announce the stranger to his master returned to tell the young magician, "Our lord wishes you to show us his image first."

Smiling, the sorcerer shook his head.

"I can show it to none," he said, "but our lord Plumed Serpent himself."

In this way he excited the penitent's curiosity, and when the page came back a second time the magician was permitted to pass.

With eyes used to the somber light of his quarters, Plumed Serpent studied the stranger's handsome face.

"What is this," he asked, "my image that you carry about with you? A man's image, his face and his heart, is a secret to all but the Lord of Duality. What can you show me?"

"Yourself," replied the magician.

The man of meditation smiled faintly. "Myself," he muttered. "And what am I? I weep. I pray. I feel pain and joy. But these are like dew that the sun dries up on the meadow. When they vanish, I am dry grass, my season passed, my little time used up. If life is a dream, what am I? If I wake again, what will I be? Is that the mysterious image you can show me?"

One by one, the magician removed the cloths that covered the object he held in his hand until he brought to light a mirror, the first Plumed Serpent had ever seen. Staring at its shining surface, Plumed Serpent drew back in horror. Many years had passed that he had not taken account of before. Forgotten was his inner self, so great was his surprise at seeing his body's reflection.

"That," he asked the magician, "is how others see me?"

The young man nodded.

The old man covered his eyes.

"I am ugly," he moaned. "My beard is like twisted fibers. My face is like rotting wood. My body is as crooked and spotty as a lizard's. What happened to my youth?" Then dashing the mirror to the floor, he cried out, "Leave my sight! Let no one look at me from this day hence!"

The magician left Plumed Serpent's cell satisfied that he had found the penitent proud and easy to injure. Plumed Serpent himself began a life of even greater seclusion than before. He had a mask made to cover his face, and no one could approach him unless he was wearing his mask.

*A drummer, as shown in the Codex Florentino*

Meanwhile, Smoking Mirror wandered at will about the city, creating havoc and causing death. Disguised as a young merchant from the Huastec Mountains, he caught the eye of the daughter of a mighty lord and so conquered her heart that she grew sick with longing for him. In the end, her father could do nothing but let her marry the hated barbarian, though their marriage caused much grumbling and ill feelings among friends, peers, and relatives. Another time Smoking Mirror sat down in the marketplace with a puppet dressed in a loincloth, cape, and collar of precious stones, and caused the puppet to dance with such lifelike grace the Toltecs trampled one another to death in their eagerness to see it. Another, Smoking Mirror arrayed himself in golden plumage and played upon a drum, calling all to dance behind him. When many had gathered, he led them outside the city, up to the cliffs, and the people in their frenzy danced over the edge, turning to stones in the ravine.

In his palace, Plumed Serpent grew weaker daily. Ill and depressed, he no longer practiced his devotions with the purity of heart he had once known. A heavy feeling of loss and failure haunted him. Where had life gone? he asked himself. Is death an escape or an ending? Does the heart of man simply vanish like the ever-withering flowers?

One day a page entered his room to say that an old man had come to see the priest-king.

"Let him come in," Plumed Serpent murmured at once. "I've been alone for many days and am becoming weary of life."

So Smoking Mirror, disguised as an ancient, was once more able to approach him.

"How are you, my son and lord?" he asked upon entering.

Plumed Serpent groaned.

"You suffer unnecessarily," the old man went on, seating himself beside the penitent. "Your body can grow young again in a flash. Your spirit can soar free. Old age and pain are illusions, as you will see upon taking the medicine I have brought you. Drink this—"

He offered Plumed Serpent a cup that he had brought hidden in his robes, but Plumed Serpent pushed it aside, saying, "I am fasting today."

"It is healthful and invigorating," the old man went on persuasively. "Recover your strength. Then you will be able to return to your saintly devotions with renewed force. A drop at least won't harm you. You'll see at once how this medicine was sent by the gods for just such as you. Dip your finger into the cup. Just taste."

His will weakened, Plumed Serpent did as the stranger urged him. Sucking his finger, he found that the liquid in the cup had a good taste and gave him the pleasant tingling of returning health. He smiled a little and said, "I will drink one cup."

But one cup was just enough to go to his head, and having finished it, he consented to another. Then he asked for a third and a fourth, shouting uproariously for the fifth. Feeling himself young and strong again, he sang and invited others to come and share his joy. "Go," he cried out to them, "and tell my sister to join us. Tell her to bring meat and fruit, for we are very merry here and even the gods do not scorn a feast!"

Obediently, Plumed Serpent's sister joined him. She, too, led a pious life, devoting her days and nights to honoring the gods in their temples. But after she had drunk Smoking Mirror's wine, she became forgetful of her duties and day passed into night without the proper ceremonies being observed. Brother and sister forgot to take the ritual bath. The sun disappeared without their knowledge, let alone their prayers. The firewood lay heaped about the altar but neither priest nor priestess set it ablaze. When dawn came, they neglected the sacrifice of quails.

Only when they had slept and awakened did they realize what foolish and sinful things they had done while their heads were muddled with wine. Plumed Serpent wept, and the bitter echo of a song he had sung the night before returned to his confused and tortured thoughts—

*Temple of the Plumed Serpent.*
*Redrawn from the Codex Nuttall*

*My house of precious plumes,*
*My house of yellow feathers,*
*My house of coral,*
*I must leave you.*
*Sorrow, sorrow!*

The song ran through his thoughts all day until at last he called together his servants and his dwarfs and gave them orders to bring wood and heap it up in his palaces, for he meant to burn them to the ground. The cacao trees that grew in his gardens he turned into thorny cactus plants. His birds with breasts of flame and tail feathers like jade he set free. In many colored clouds they rose above the clouds of smoke, and following in their wake, Plumed Serpent turned his footsteps toward the rainlands and the country of boats. Outside the city, he paused a moment under a tall, thick-trunked tree and asked his page for a mirror.

"Yes," he nodded, no longer afraid of what he saw reflected there, "I am old."

Then he departed toward the east, leaving Tula to Smoking Mirror. And when he reached the sea after a long time of wandering, he set out on the waters alone, on a raft of serpents, bound for the red and black Land of Wisdom. But others say that when he came to the coast he set himself afire and that all the birds of the sky flocked to see his sacrifice. When the flames died down, Plumed Serpent's heart rose out of the ashes and soared up to heaven, where it became the sun's companion, the morning star.

*Dwarfish water carrier. A sculpture in clay from the west coast of Mexico*

# The King and the Rain Dwarfs

In a pleasant land somewhere in the warm south lived Tlaloc, the rain god. His was a land of leafy willows and fruit trees, budding green meadows and brightly flowered hillsides, of golden mists and mauve-tinted showers. There were lakes and rivers, waterfalls and swimming pools. Those fortunate enough to live in Tlalocan spent their days at water sports, hunting butterflies, or gathering flowers, playing games and dancing. Many of them were children.

Tlaloc also had a palace built high up in the mountains where clouds gathered even at midday. The palace was gloomy, perhaps, but it served a purpose. In a large courtyard stood four immense tubs of water. The water in the first tub was the rain that falls in season, causing the earth to green and bear fruit. The water in the second tub was rain that falls out of season, causing plants to mildew. The water in the third tub produced hail. And the water in the fourth made plants dry up.

All this water had to be sprinkled about the earth at the rain god's orders, and the task was carried out by innumerable dwarfs—red dwarfs, white dwarfs, yellow dwarfs, and blue dwarfs. Mischievous as puppies and quick as the wind that scatters leaves before a storm, they ran about from hilltop to hilltop carrying water jars balanced on their heads, backs, or shoulders. For really good rainstorms the jars went crashing down to earth along with flashes of lightning and terrible rolls of thunder.

The rain dwarfs were also ball players.

Now there was once a king of Tula who challenged them to a game on his great, H-shaped ball court.

Such a challenge was not to be taken lightly, for many a player could die in the scuffle. But the dwarfs knew no fear.

"What will you bet?" they asked, the ball game also being an excuse to gamble.

And the king, confident of victory, replied, "My most precious jade and quetzal plumes."

The dwarfs accepted this wager. "If you win," they said, "we will give you the same."

At one end of the court the king and his team of tall athletes put on gloves, hip-guards, and leg-guards. At the other end the tiny dwarfs stood ready, waiting for the hard rubber ball to be thrown out. Then back and forth the two teams charged, trying to drive the ball through one of two stone rings suspended on the high walls edging the court.

At one moment the dwarfs seemed to have the advantage, being so small they could scamper between the taller players' legs. The next moment the king's men appeared to be winning, they were so light on their feet and so ready with their knees. It was forbidden to touch the ball in motion with hands or feet. Elbows and knees were supposed to drive the ball, but sometimes smashed into faces and caught

*A ball player. A sculpture
in clay from Jalisco*

unwary opponents in the stomach. Many players had
the wind knocked out of them, too, when the solid
rubber ball hit them flat on the back or square on the
chest, and others were scraped on the gravel after
slipping, or being pushed. Finally, at the game's end,
bruised and breathless, the king's men were the win-
ners.

"The wager!" called out the king to the dwarfs, his
voice booming with pride.

But instead of precious stones the dwarfs gave him
grains of corn, and instead of shining plumes they
gave him corn leaves.

The king scowled.

"What are these?" he demanded. "Are they the jade and quetzal feathers I have won?"

The dwarfs replied, "Take them. They are the most precious things we can give you."

But the king threw the corn on the ground in disdain and, turning away, strode back to his palace.

"Very well," muttered the dwarfs among themselves. "We will hide what you hold to be of so little value."

As soon as they reached the cloud palace of Tlaloc, they made a shower of hail that blackened the sky and whitened the ground about Tula. Crops froze. The earth froze. Then followed months of heat so intense even stones split open. Dried corn leaves rattled like bones in the fields. Year after year, famine plagued the people of Tula, who sacrificed prisoners of war to no avail. The rain god's anger would not be appeased. Many parents were forced to sell their children into slavery to buy food.

At the end of four years, a Toltec who was wandering about the Aztec city of Tenochtitlan came upon a fountain that gushed out of the Hill of the Grasshopper. He saw an ear of corn floating in the water.

Amazed at first, he picked up the corn and began to munch the raw grains. All at once, as though he had risen out of the water itself, a priest of the rain god stood beside him.

"Do you know what you have in your hands?" the priest cried out angrily.

"Yes, lord," replied the starving Toltec. "Years have passed since we lost this in my city."

Then the priest of the rain god told him, "Take the corn to your king and tell him to ask the Aztecs for the little girl called Flower of the Precious Plume. She must be drowned in the rain god's pool before your people will cease to be hungry. But it must be the Aztec girl and no child of the Toltecs, for the days of Tula are numbered."

Quickly the man returned to his own city and repeated all that he had seen and heard, and the king of Tula sent ambassadors to Tenochtitlan, asking for the little girl who alone could bring an end to the famine. For four days the Aztecs fasted and mourned her. On the fifth day her father, who had often called her his bracelet of precious stones, took her to the well of sacrifice. And as soon as the child's soul reached Tlalocan and joined in the games and dancing

*Tlaloc, the rain god, as shown in a*
*colored clay sculpture from Tula*

there, the sky above Tula clouded over. For four days and nights rain fell. The muddy earth greened. The harvest that year yielded twenty to forty times what it had yielded in any year within the memory of man.

*A heron. Redrawn from a Veracruz flat stamp*

# People of the
# Heron and the Hummingbird

"Teewee, teewee, teewee," sang a bird in the White Land. Day after day the people of the Seven Caves heard its song, always the same—"Teewee, teewee, teewee." At first they laughed because "Teewee" resembled the word in their language that meant "Let's go." Then tribe after tribe became restless, leaving the Seven Caves for a life of wandering, to follow a dream that drew them farther and farther south.

The tribe that called itself the Aztecs—People of the White Land or Heron People—was the last to leave the Seven Caves. Like a tardy flock of birds with winter at their backs, they scurried toward the mountains, beyond which the other tribes had long disappeared. Being the last did not mean they were less confident of their future. Their god, Hummingbird of the South, whose image they carried with them, had promised to guide them to a land of their own.

Hummingbird of the South spoke to his priests at night, in their dreams. At times his instructions were hard to carry out, for with green forests and grassy plains on all sides and nothing but desert in the distance, the people hesitated to move on. In some places they stayed long enough to build towns and temples and the most reluctant among them remained behind, though the rest gave in to the proddings of their god. One story tells how the group which later founded the Tarascan nation chose to stay on the shores of a fish-filled lake. While they were bathing in its waters, those who were determined to go on stole the swimmers' clothes and left them to enjoy their paradise naked as fish.

*An Aztec dignitary, as pictured*
*in the Codex Mendocino*

Whenever hardships undermined the faith of his followers, Hummingbird of the South renewed the vision he had given them. One night when they were camped on a hill above a dusty plain, the god spoke to his priests.

"I will show you what you can expect to find when you reach the place I have promised you," he said. And he told the priests to dam a narrow river that flowed through the plain so the lowland would fill up with water and make a lake below the hill. Once the lake was made, willows, cypresses, and poplars grew up along its shore. Rushes and reeds dressed the edge of the lake and fish, frogs, and water fowl came to live among the water lilies. There seemed to be nothing more a homeless tribe could go on seeking.

As had happened before, the road-weary wanderers delayed departure until the days turned into months. A city grew up on the hill and certain people began to whisper in their prayers, "Here is your home, Hummingbird of the South, here on Serpent Mountain. We will give you precious stones and shining feathers, rich cloaks and cacao, if you will only command your priests to say this is the promised land."

But the god grew angry when he heard these words. One midnight the silence was broken by cries that came from the ball court and from the skull rack near the temple of the god. When morning came, those who had been foremost in urging the god to let them remain were found dead, their bodies split open and their hearts torn out.

Then Hummingbird of the South ordered the dam to be destroyed. The waters of the lake dried up and the trees withered. Fish, frogs, and water fowl died in the dust, leaving the people without food. Setting out from that place, the Aztecs did not look back. Dry winds scattered sand over their tracks and the desert showed no sign that they had ever stayed there.

Quarrels, however, went with the wanderers. There were still those among them who prevented the people from living at peace with one another, and chief among the troublemakers was a woman named Wild Grass Flower. Beautiful and sharp-witted, she was so powerful in the tribe that people called her the sister of Hummingbird of the South. Smoking Mirror, though, was her god. At night she read the stars and listened to the hooting of owls until she was skilled in witchcraft and could, by incantation, command animals and insects to do her will. Anyone who opposed her died by the bites of scorpions, centipedes, snakes, or spiders. Living in fear of her, the people begged the priests to rid the tribe of her presence.

One morning the witch found herself abandoned with a few of her followers. About them rose sheer cliffs and pinnacles of rock. Wild animals peered down at them from caves in the jagged walls. There was nothing to point the way the tribe had gone, stealing off while the witch and her friends had been asleep. Weeping angrily at being left behind, Wild Grass Flower swore revenge.

*Aztec sculpture of a grasshopper*

Children who were only toddling at that time were men and women with children of their own when the Aztecs finally reached the Hill of the Grasshopper on the shores of Lake Texcoco. Many who had set out from the Seven Caves were dead. Only the very oldest members of the tribe remembered the White Land.

The Aztecs were half afraid to settle on the Hill of the Grasshopper because the shores of the lake were dotted with the cities of tribes that had left the Seven Caves in advance of Hummingbird's people. Building huts, as they had built them a hundred times before in as many places, they felt they were surrounded by enemies. To protect themselves, they chose a war leader, and under his command they fortified the hill, repaired broken weapons, and made new ones.

The danger they felt was not imagined. Among those who had grown to manhood since the tribe deserted Wild Grass Flower was the witch's own son, Copil. Growing up in that land of cliffs and caves where his mother was forced to make her home, he had been nursed throughout his childhood on the poison of her hatred for the people who had abandoned her. As a youth he had wandered from city to city, always speaking ill of the Aztecs and kindling hatred against them.

"They will come," he told the cities on the lake, "and take your towns. They will rob you of your land and burn your temples and make your people slaves or sacrificial victims. They are barbarians who know nothing but how to kill and take what does not belong to them."

By the time the Aztecs arrived at the Hill of the Grasshopper, all the towns of the lake were alarmed and determined not to let them remain in that country. Hummingbird of the South, through his priests, warned his people of the trouble. The towns of the lake were forming a league to destroy the Aztecs, and Copil was somewhere nearby to watch his mother's enemies put to slaughter. Copil's hiding place, however, was known to the god, and he instructed the Aztecs how to find him and what to do.

Acting before the league was ready for battle, Aztec warriors stole up the hill Copil had chosen for his lair and captured him. As was their custom with a prisoner, they tore out his heart and presented it to their god, but Hummingbird of the South did not want it burned.

"Take it," he said, "and standing in the reeds at the edge of the lake, one of you must cast the heart into the middle of the lake with all your strength."

And so it was done, just as the god commanded.

Copil's death, however, did not put an end to the war plans made by the league of lake cities. The Aztecs had to defend themselves in battle after battle, and though they fought valiantly, they were forced to move from place to place for greater security. It seemed their wanderings would never end. But the first sign of fulfillment of their god's promise finally came.

One day they found a juniper tree as white as a heron's wing. A spring of clear water gushed out of the ground at its roots, and just beyond it stood a grove of willows on which there was not one green leaf. Both bark and foliage were as white as the juniper. The cattails in that place were white also, and white frogs and fish lived among them. Seeing these wonders, the Aztecs thought of their homeland and took heart, knowing that they were approaching their new home.

The next night Hummingbird of the South appeared in dreams to the priests, saying, "Now you will see that I have been telling you the truth. Remember I told you to throw the heart of your enemy Copil into the lake, and you obeyed my command. Now, his heart fell on a stone where it lay decaying until it provided the earth for a prickly pear cactus seed to sprout. The cactus has now grown so tall an eagle has made his nest on it out of the colored feathers of the birds on which he feeds. Each day, standing on his nest, he stretches out his wings to receive the warmth of the sun. And there, where the eagle is, my people too will feel the sun's love and good will. Go to the Place of the Prickly Pear Cactus, Tenochtitlan, and found there a city with that name. That is the homeland I have promised you, and Tenochtitlan will be queen of all cities in the land."

A long time had passed since the incident of Copil's heart, and the Aztecs no longer knew where to look for it. But returning to the place where they had seen

*The eagle on the cactus. From an*
*Aztec stone carving*

the white juniper, they found everything changed.
Trees and reeds were normal colors now, while the
spring of clear water had divided in two. One stream
was red as blood while the other was blue as the waters of the rain god. From there the Aztecs caught
sight of the giant cactus they had been told to seek.
And the eagle was standing on his nest, spreading
his wings in the sun.

# MAYAN MYTHS

*A flute player. From the Codex Dresden*

# The Monkey Musicians

There was once an old woman, perhaps the first old woman that ever was, who lived in the woods with her grandsons. Except for her, they would have had no one to look after them, but they were an ungrateful pair just the same. They never helped their grandmother with the work and seldom helped themselves. Day in, day out, they sang or danced or played the flute, finding time for nothing else.

One afternoon while the grandmother was working, a shadow fell inside the hut, and looking up,
the old woman saw a girl. Up until that time, at least
for as long as her grandsons had been living with her,
she had hardly seen anyone but them. So instead of
being glad to see a new face, she was frightened. She
knew at once that trouble lay ahead.

The girl, standing in the doorway waiting for the
grandmother to speak first, finally broke the silence
herself.

"I am your daughter-in-law," she said.

Imagine the old woman's thoughts at hearing such
words, no stranger than the sound of rain, yet dreadful because so unexpected. Besides, the girl was not
alone. Attending her were four owls rather larger
than owls usually are, with eyes like moons and
beaks like eagles' talons. Terrible as they looked, they
seemed to be devoted to the girl, and she showed no
fear of them. But the old woman saw everything new
as an evil omen.

Once, of course, the old woman had not been old.
She had had a husband and sons. One of her sons
had married and was the father of her grandsons. But
his wife had died and both he and his brother had dis-

*A Mayan thatched-roof house, as shown*
*in a frieze at Uxmal*

appeared so long ago that the old woman had long
grown accustomed to thinking of them as dead.

"You are not my daughter-in-law," she told the
girl in the doorway.

Tears glistened on the stranger's cheeks.

"Your sons are dead," she wept, "sacrificed in the
kingdom where my father is a powerful lord, but
here I am, your son's wife. It was his own wish that
I come here."

If the old woman was not pleased at having a
daughter-in-law, she was even less pleased when
twin boys were born shortly after the girl's arrival,
making still more mouths to feed. The girl worked
hard, but neither she nor her children were allowed
to live in the hut. The flute players, the old woman's
first grandsons, also disliked intruders. So the twins

grew up in the woods, taught by the owls who served their mother.

One boy was called Little Jaguar and the other Blowgun Hunter, and both could hunt like jaguars and bring down game with their blowguns. But the game they shot and brought home went to feed the flute players, while the twins gnawed the bones, ate fruit, and kept their thoughts to themselves. The owls' wisdom taught them to be patient and, also, to have no doubts about their destiny.

One day when the twins were almost grown to young men, they returned from the woods without any game. Their grandmother scolded them furiously.

"Why didn't you bring any birds?" she demanded. "Your stepbrothers are hungry!"

"All the birds we shot, dozens of them, caught in the branches of a giant tree," the twins explained. "Perhaps if our stepbrothers would like to come and help us, we can shake the birds down and have plenty to eat."

So off went the four young men down a trail that led to the heart of the forest. At last they came to a tall tree so full of birds they looked like fruit hanging on its branches.

"Climb up and shake them down," said the twins to the stepbrothers. "We'll pick them up and carry them home."

The flute players mounted the lowest branches. They were naked except for loincloths tied about their waists, and though they were not used to climbing, they got from one branch to another clumsily but with success. Still, as high as they climbed, the birds always seemed to be just beyond their reach. At last, swaying high above the ground, they called down to the twins for help.

"You tricked us," they shouted. "The birds must be hanging from the clouds."

But Little Jaguar and Blowgun Hunter called back, "You're almost on top of them! Untie your loincloths and arrange them so that one end hangs way down behind you like a tail. That way you can move about more easily and without fear."

Grudgingly, the brothers in the tree loosened their loincloths and let one end hang down behind like a tail. And it was true, from then on they could move smoothly from branch to branch because their loincloths turned into real tails by which they could swing. Moreover, their arms and legs turned into spindly limbs, and their faces into monkey faces. Instead of climbing after the birds or coming back to the ground, the flute players vanished into the forest howling shrill monkey cries.

The twins returned home, where their grandmother wanted to know what had happened to her favorites, who had gone into the forest with them.

"Don't worry, little grandmother," her grandsons told her. "They'll come back. But when they do, remember this—if you laugh at them, they'll go away forever and you will never see them again."

Then they took up the idle flutes and began to play a merry air. It was not long before the sound of music reached the new monkeys' ears and brought them to the open door. In they peered, their wrinkled features moved by the music of which they were so fond. Their noses twitched. Their woeful eyes blinked tears. Their elastic lips twisted and curled. Their grandmother laughed.

Twice the monkeys fled to the woods. Twice they returned. But as they could not help waving their arms about and dancing with the oddest antics when they heard the flutes, their grandmother's laughter rang out again and again. At last they fled to return no more.

*The monkey god of music. From a*
*Mayan carving*

The grandmother was inconsolable. Where she had been helpless to keep a straight face, now she wept. But her tears were for gods, for gods the idle flute players became—the monkey gods of musicians, singers and dancers, sculptors, painters, goldsmiths and silversmiths, and all who practice the arts.

*A jaguar. From a Mayan stone carving*

# Xibalba

Ax bit tree. With one blow, tree and vine fell crashing to earth though no hand grasped the ax's handle. Pick chewed earth, spitting stone, thistles, and uprooted boles to one side of the clearing. A hoe munched the larger morsels left by pick, preparing the earth for planting, while its masters lay in the shade shooting pellets from their blowguns at any target they fancied.

At noon a bird sang out to warn the twins. Blowgun Hunter and Little Jaguar leaped to their feet and seized a tool apiece. When their grandmother came in sight with their midday meal, they were hard at work, chopping and breaking up the ground. They ate without having worked, and yet the work was done.

Done in vain, however, for the next morning when they returned to the field, every tree was standing and every stone gone back to the soil. Thistles and vines had rewoven their nets.

"Who played this trick on us?" the twins asked each other. And after clearing the field again that day, they went home only to return that night to see who would come to make fun of them and undo their work. Hiding themselves, they waited. At midnight they heard voices, and then came the animals, one of each kind, saying in his own language, "Rise up, trees. Rise up, vines." And the vines and trees obeyed.

Blowgun Hunter and Little Jaguar sprang out of their hiding place, lunging and leaping after the treacherous animals. They tried to seize the puma and the jaguar, but the fleet animals escaped. The coyote, the wild boar, and the coati passed through their hands like water. They were able to catch the deer and the rabbit only by their tails, and even those animals broke away, leaving most of their tails in the twins' hands, running off into the forest with only a tuft, such as they have to this day.

But the rat did not get away, and to punish it, the twins burned its tail in a fire, which is why the rat's tail has been hairless ever since. Nevertheless, the rat saved its life by crying out, "I am not destined to die by your hands, nor is it your destiny to be farmers. Let me go and I will tell you something."

"What is it?" asked the twins, loosening their grip on the little rat.

"Foolish boys," said the rat, giving itself a shake. "You know your father and your uncle did not plant corn. They spent their days playing ball. The lords of Xibalba, hearing the noise they made overhead, said to themselves, 'Let us challenge those two to play ball with us. When they lose, we will sacrifice them.' And so it came to pass. But before they went to Xibalba, your father left his ball and his playing gear hidden in the rafters of your grandmother's house. There they lie hidden to this day. If you want to avenge the deaths of your father and your uncle, you must forget about farm tools and get the ball and playing gear down."

Overjoyed at what the rat told them, the twins replied, "Little rat, you shall have a reward for this information. From now on, corn, beans, seeds, everything that is stored shall be your rightful food."

Then they lost no time in searching the rafters of the house until they found the equipment their father had hidden there. Each day thereafter, they went to play ball on the old ball court their father and uncle had cleared, making so much noise the lords of Xibalba could not help asking one another, "Who is making that thunder roll over our heads? Is it possible the sons are ready to meet their father's fate?"

And each day the twins awaited a summons to the underworld.

The twins, now grown to manhood, were dearly loved by the grandmother who once cared nothing for them. She worked for them as devotedly as she had worked for their stepbrothers, the flute players, and when the owl messengers of Xibalba arrived at last with the news that the twins had been summoned there, the old woman's heart was chilled with fear.

"This is how their father and uncle were summoned," she remembered. "And the twins will be murdered there, just as they were. Who can I send to them with such terrible news?"

And as she sat mulling these thoughts in her mind, a louse fell into her lap.

"Will you go?" she asked. So the willing louse set off for the playing field with the message. But as it went swaggering along, it caught the attention of a toad.

"Where are you going?"

"To the ball court. I have a message for the twins."

"I see," said the toad. "But you'll get where you're going more rapidly if I carry you. Shall I swallow you?"

Unafraid, the louse consented to be swallowed and off leaped the toad. Having gone but a short distance, however, the toad was stopped by a snake.

"Where are you going?"

"To the ball court. I carry a message in my stomach."

"Good. But you'll travel faster if I carry you. Jump into my mouth."

The toad followed the snake's suggestion and away

they slithered, only to be caught and swallowed by a hawk.

Blowgun Hunter and Little Jaguar were playing ball when they heard the hawk screaming overhead and interrupted their game to shoot down the noisy bird. Then the hawk loosed the snake and the snake loosed the toad, but the toad could not loose the louse because the tiny insect was not in its stomach. The louse had hidden behind one of the toad's teeth. Thus the hawk and the snake discovered their natural food, but the toad was left wondering.

"Is it true?" the twins asked their grandmother when they arrived home.

The old woman wept as she nodded, reaching out to embrace them.

"Then we must go," the twins told her. "Our destiny is plain." And as she seemed unwilling or unable to let them depart, they planted two green reeds in the earth floor of the house and said, "Look, these are the sign of our fate. Watching them grow, you will always know how we fare, whether we are alive or dead. If you see the reeds dry up, you will know we are dead. But if they sprout again, you will know we are living. Now let us go, for you have this to comfort you."

When they were gone, the grandmother continued to mourn her loss, fearing she would never see her grandsons again. Day after day she watered the reeds to keep them fresh and green, but one morning she awoke to find them yellow as straw. Then she knew the worst had happened and her heart nearly broke. Still, remembering the twins' last words, she watched the reeds for four more days. On the fifth day, new shoots appeared at the bottom of the stalks. Wondering and rejoicing at their appearance, the grandmother tended them as carefully as though they had human life.

Far underground, in Xibalba, the twins had passed test after test and avoided trap after trap prepared for them by the demons and lords of the dead. In the great hall of the lords sat two lifelike figures made of wood. Years before, the twins' father and uncle had greeted them as though they were true lords of Xibalba and by that mistake sealed their own fate, but Little Jaguar and Blowgun Hunter saw through the lifelike paint to the wood of the statues and passed them by in silence.

*The Lord of the Dead. From a Totonac sculpture*

Neither did the twins die in the House of Gloom, the House of Flying Knives, the House of Freezing Winds, the House of Jaguars, the House of Fire, or the House of Vampire Bats. Nor did they die on the ball-playing field. In fact, by driving their ball through their opponents' ring, they won the game and deprived the lords of Xibalba of their last pretext for putting them to death. Nevertheless, they allowed the lords to sacrifice them in a raging bonfire. It was part of their plan to defeat the demons and avenge their father's death. When they were burned, the reeds they had left in the house of their grandmother turned yellow and dried up.

*A dancer disguised as a bird. From a Mayan sculpture*

Five days later, two vagabonds appeared in the marketplace of Xibalba. At first they attracted attention to themselves with clever imitations of animals. They did the owl dance, the weasel dance, the armadillo dance, and a dance on stilts, the laughter of the spectators drawing a large crowd.

When all the people in the marketplace had gathered around to watch them, the vagabonds began performing feats of magic so startling they could hardly be believed. They caused houses to blaze up before everyone's eyes. But when they had burned to the ground, they revealed to one and all that the fire had been but an illusion, a dream the vagabonds had caused everyone to dream, and the houses were unharmed. The people of Xibalba watched with still greater wonder as the performers killed one another and cut each other up with knives. But this, too, was shown to be an illusion, a waking dream, and neither vagabond was hurt.

Word spread quickly from the marketplace to the palace where the lords of Xibalba were sitting.

"Everything they do is more marvelous than we have ever seen," ran the rumor, until the curious lords sent to have the vagabonds brought before them.

"But we are poor and ugly," protested the performers when they heard the summons. "Look at us. We are not fit to appear before great lords." And they were so reluctant to go to the palace they had to be driven there with rods.

In the presence of the lords, they hung their heads and gave vague answers to questions about themselves. But when they began to dance, as they were told to do, the people of the palace were as amused as the people of the marketplace had been.

"Cut my dog in pieces and bring him back to life!" one of the lords commanded, eager to see the magic that had been described to him. And after they had done what he said, the dog was as full of life as it had been before.

Then another lord ordered them to burn his house. From the window of the palace everyone watched it go up in flames. The roof and walls collapsed. But then, in an instant, the flames disappeared and the house was seen to be standing with no sign of smoke or cinders.

All the lords were amazed and pleased. One after another they asked for more tricks to astound their eyes.

"Tear out a man's heart and then restore him to life!"

"Sacrifice yourselves!"

Everything the vagabonds did was beyond belief, yet it was all illusion, the result of the way they manipulated their hands and eyes.

"Now sacrifice us!" the enthusiastic lords clamored at last.

So at their bidding the two vagabonds slew the two principal lords, One Dead and Seven Dead, and tore

*An owl, pictured on a stone yoke from Tajín*

out their hearts. But what they did this time was not an illusion. What they did could not be undone. The lords were truly dead.

Then the twins revealed their identity to everyone assembled there. They drove the people of the owl land into ravines and deprived them of their riches and their rank, bringing about an end to their empire. Thus they avenged the death of their father and their uncle.

In her house, their grandmother watched the green reeds steadily grow.

# MYTHS OF THE INHERITORS

*The sun bird sitting on a weaver's loom,*
*as pictured in an ancient Mayan sculpture*

# Brother Sun and Sister Moon
## *A Mixe Myth*

Watching Maria was like watching a hummingbird, so quickly did she work. Seated on the ground, a loom fastened to a strap that went around her narrow back, she made the bobbins dart in and out like fish swimming among reeds, weaving two, three, four colors into a blanket or wrap-around skirt. Her fingers on the batten flew faster than an eye could see and the web grew upward as if it were alive.

Maria was proud of her weaving. Her knots were small, her lines even, her yarn clean. One day when a small bird fluttered down and sat on her warp beam, looking at her with a kind of silent challenge, she whisked it away at once, worried it might spoil her work.

In a minute the bird returned, hopping from one thread to another.

"You naughty thing, what are you doing?" cried Maria angrily. "Why are you getting my threads dirty?"

And when it returned a third time, lighting on her loom as before, she lost her temper, pulled out the batten, and struck at its head. She was surprised herself that the bird did not escape the blow, and as it fell and rolled down the threads toward her, she picked it up and put it inside her blouse, next to her skin, thinking it might revive with warmth.

After some time the bird began moving about. Its claws scratched a bit but its whisking wings felt like another heart beating against her own and made Maria happy until a sharp peck made her gasp with pain.

"Now I will kill you!" she cried out, but the clever

bird slipped between her hasty fingers and flew away. After a short time had passed, Maria discovered she was to become a mother.

Some months later, Maria went into the woods looking for twigs and branches. Here and there she walked, singing as she picked up one stick after another. Some were green with moss, some were grayish-white with fungus, some were black as though they had been burned. Their colors pleased her. She felt her spirits soar. And then she saw something that made her burst out laughing. Up among the leaves of the trees a squirrel was swinging in the loop of a vine.

"What are you doing?" she cried out, holding her sides with laughter as the little animal swung back and forth in ever-widening arcs, flicking its tail right and left to keep its balance.

"It's fun," the squirrel called down to her. "Don't you want to try?"

Another day Maria would not have dared, but she was in the mood to dare that day.

"Can you push me?" she asked the squirrel saucily.

"Come on up and see," he chattered back.

Dropping her bundle, Maria climbed the tree as

though she were an animal herself, and the squirrel made the loop in the vine a little larger so that she could sit in it. Then he gave her a push. Her feet reached out and touched the branches of other trees. With a second push, they kicked above the treetops, in the face of the sun itself. But the third push sent her flying through the air, then hurtling, hurtling downward. When she struck the ground, her bones broke.

Hearing the noise, a vulture turning circles overhead flew quickly to the spot, skidding as it touched earth, dragging its wings to a stop at Maria's side. But before it could tear her flesh with its hungry beak, a voice cried out from inside her body, "It's not time for you to eat yet! Make a neat cut, not too deep, and you will see!"

Bewildered but obedient, the vulture made a neat opening above the place from which the voice came, and out jumped Maria's children, a boy and a girl.

"Now," said the boy to the vulture, "you must fly three times around that mountain over there, and when you do that, then it will be time for you to eat."

Amazed, off flew the vulture, and the boy worked rapidly to bury his mother in the earth. Then he flung

*A vulture. Redrawn from the Codex Dresden*

her shawl over a large stone and, taking his sister's hand, ran away as fast as their legs would move. When the vulture returned from making three quick turns above the mountaintop, it sighted the shawl lying on the ground below and, thinking it was Maria's body, dropped like lightning. What a blow when it struck the stone! Ever since that day all vultures' beaks have been a sore-looking red.

Running, the children reached the house of their grandmother, a wicked woman who took them in only because she saw they were strong enough to work hard. Brother was sent out to hunt game, while Sister was kept busy sweeping, scrubbing, spinning, and grinding corn. At night they went to bed hungry, for all the food in the house went to feed an ogre who came to visit the grandmother daily. While the exhausted children slept, the old woman smeared their lips with fat. Then when they woke up and asked for something to eat, she scolded them, "Look at those greasy faces, and you mean to tell me you haven't eaten! If you want to stuff yourselves, work harder!"

"We must run away," Brother told Sister one day when their grandmother had gone down to the river to gather herbs. "This is not the life we were born to lead."

But before they left the house, Brother used his bow and arrows to kill the ogre, who was asleep under a blanket on a straw mat near the fire. Then Brother filled a deerskin with stinging insects and covered it up with the same blanket. By the time the old woman came back, the children were gone and the ogre was still snoring—at least she thought he was snoring when she heard the drone and buzz of the wasps and bees sewn into the deerskin.

"Get up," she grumbled, nudging the bulk under the blanket. "Get up, lazybones!"

And when the supposed ogre did not move, she lost patience and gave him such a kick she broke the deerskin and let all the stinging insects loose. Before she could reach the river and duck herself, she was as covered with swellings as a toad.

Nevertheless, her painful bites did not prevent the old woman from pursuing the children who had tricked her.

Brother heard her coming after them just as he and Sister were passing a woman washing turkey grass in a stream.

"Hide us!" they begged her. And the woman, seeing how frightened and helpless they were, looked about the flat countryside for some place to conceal them, but she looked in vain.

"There's nowhere," she told them. "Run on as fast as you can."

But Brother and Sister made themselves small as two bird's eggs and hid themselves in the woman's mouth, one in one cheek and one in the other. When their grandmother came to the stream, panting and perspiring in her haste, she sat down by the woman, who was still washing turkey grass.

"What are you doing?" asked the grandmother when she had caught her breath again.

"Washing," replied the woman, unable to say another word with her mouth so full.

"Haven't you seen two children go by here?" the grandmother asked.

The woman kneeling by the water only shook her head and went on with her work.

To lose no more time, the grandmother got up and wearily hobbled off. When she was out of sight, the children came out of their hiding place, growing to their natural height once more. Then for three days Brother burrowed in the ground with a stick, and after he had made a good many tunnels, he turned the kind washwoman into a mole with cheeks puffed out as if she always had her mouth full.

Nothing but unhappiness, however, seemed to be in store for the children on earth, so Brother climbed up to the sky. Until that time, there had been no light on earth, but as Brother climbed upward, he began to shine as though he had set himself on fire, and he gave both light and warmth to the earth. Sister dogged his footsteps as usual, used as she was to following with her hand in his, but the time had come for them to separate.

To lose her, Brother asked her to go back to earth for his sandal, which he had left behind. Sister obeyed,

*The Mayan sun god, as pictured in a
stone carving from Cozumel*

but ran and ran across the sky until she had caught up with him again. Then Brother took off his other sandal and threw it in her face, leaving a dark bruise on her white cheek. After that, she did not tag him as closely as before. Still, every now and then the moon almost catches up with the sun, and then you can see Brother and Sister in the sky at the same time.

*A cornstalk. Redrawn from a Huichol yarn painting*

# The Aunts
## *A Huichol Myth*

Two. Only two were left alive when the first ray of sun broke through the rain clouds hugging the flooded earth. Two people amidst the fallen forests, fields of mud, and ponds filled with the debris of death. The Worker and his mother disembarked from their boat, feet sinking in the ooze.

In time the land dried and began to dress itself anew. Then, as before the flood, the Worker struggled with the forest for a living. He and his mother built a hut in a clearing made by ants. Beans and squash were their only food, and they often went hungry.

At night the Worker's stomach rolled with hunger. At the same time he could hear sounds from the nearby anthill, sounds of cooking and feasting and cries of "Health!" and the laughter that goes hand in hand with full stomachs. One night the Worker rose from his straw mat and spied on the ants. From the way they were roasting and eating and drinking, he saw there was no scarcity of corn in the anthill.

But the Worker was too embarrassed to ask the ants how they got their corn. He could not admit to them that he and his mother were starving while there was plenty of food next door. Yet he could not sleep thinking about his hunger.

"Mother," he said at last, "speak to our aunts, our neighbors in the anthill. Ask them to tell you where corn can be found. They helped us clear our land. They always seem friendly. And I notice you gossip with them. I know they have plenty of food because the noise of their feasting keeps me awake at night. Ask them how we can find corn too."

Obedient to her son's wishes, the Worker's mother pulled her shawl over her head and went out to speak to their busy neighbors, begging their pardon for her curiosity.

"Don't be foolish!" the lady ants replied. "Why didn't you ask sooner? Aren't we neighbors? Aren't we friends? If we had known you were starving, we would have asked you to join us. There's plenty of food for all. It comes from a pretty white house where they have corn in five colors. More than you've ever seen before. There's no need for anyone to go hungry."

"It's bound to cost a lot," the Worker's mother said. But the ants laughed merrily at her fears.

"Cost!" they giggled. "Cost indeed! Why, we buy it with hay or kindling and bits of broken jars. If you like, come with us. We'll take you to the pretty white house."

"My son will go with you, if you'll be so kind as to take him," the woman said. "And we're grateful for your kindness."

"Not at all, not at all! We're your aunts and we're here to serve you," chorused the busy little ladies.

The next day the Worker and the ants went off

together. The ants were as lighthearted as ever, joking about how handsome the Worker was, and still unmarried.

"Remember," they told him, "we're not all your aunts. Some of us are your sweet little cousins!" And they laughed when his face turned red.

"Did you bring something along to buy the corn?" they asked. And when he showed what he had brought, they giggled again. But they were always giggling about something.

Before they reached their journey's end, night fell.

"Sleepy time!" said the ants, and they lay down without another word. The Worker sat up awhile, thinking about the strange little creatures with whom he was traveling. What fun-loving companions they were, always working, yet always making a game of it. Then he too lay down on his side and slept.

While he was sleeping, the ants did their mischief. Giggling and whispering, joking and bustling, they plucked every hair of his head and eyebrows, leaving him bald as a stone. They even plucked his eyelashes, then disappeared like a party of thieves.

The morning sun burned the Worker's eyes like hot needles when he awoke. Passing his hand over

*A dove. Redrawn from a Huichol embroidery design*

the top of his shaven head, he felt as if he had been robbed of his clothes. Where to hide was his first thought. He did not know if he dared go home again. Then fear and disgrace gave way to anger. Enraged at having let the ants take him for a fool, he struck at trees with his fists, bellowing with rage.

The voice of a dove calmed him at last.

"Cucurrucu! What happened?" she asked so softly his rage gave way to tears. "Why are you behaving like a wild bull?"

"Ah," she exclaimed sympathetically when he had told her all. "Those wicked ants! Those liars and thieves! How well I know them. So they told you they come here to buy corn with broken jars and kindling and hay? They come here to steal it and those are the things we throw at them to chase them away! Come," she said, "let me take you home. You need something to eat and you will meet my daughters. Maybe one of them will like you well enough to cheer you up."

Led to a small white house nearby, the Worker was surprised to see overflowing bins of corn there. Yet the dove gave him only a small flat corn cake and a tiny jug of gruel to eat. When the Worker saw them, he thought they would only make him hungrier. But when he had eaten all he could, there was still a piece of the flat cake and some of the gruel left over. The dove, he realized then, was the corn mother.

After he had eaten, the dove called to her daughters and they stood, with downcast eyes, before the young man. They were the prettiest girls he had ever seen. One was robed in blue, one in yellow, one in red, one in white, and one wore a speckled dress. Each girl's hair fell thick to her waist, and their sandals were as green as young plants.

Then their mother said to the Worker, "Why don't you take one of them home with you? The one in blue—do you like her?"

But the Worker shook his head. "There is not

enough in our house to feed my mother and myself,"
he said. "How could I feed a wife too?"

But the dove laughed, very sweetly. "My daughter," she said, "will provide. As long as she lives
with you, there will be all the corn you can eat in
your house. But you must promise me one thing.
Never make her work. Do you hear that? She must
never work. Promise me that and she is yours."

His promise given, the Worker took the girl and
returned home. In a short time he and his mother
had more corn than they could eat. More than they
could store. More than they could plant. Ears of corn
hung from the ceiling and the eaves of their house.
Their silos were full. Ears of corn were piled up every-
where. Baskets overflowed with corn. Sacks of seed
bulged like fat men after a feast. The mother's arms
ached from husking corn, grinding corn, patting corn
meal into flat cakes. The Worker felled forests to clear
field after field. He sowed mountainsides and mountain valleys. He reaped more than he could store, but
still some rotted on the ground.

Meanwhile, the girl in blue sat doing nothing.

The Worker had made a little altar for her and
there she sat, combing her hair among the beaded

*Plant design from a Huichol beaded bowl*

offering bowls and incense burners, or weaving garlands of field flowers. Twenty times a day the Worker's mother passed the girl and twenty times a day she noticed her idleness. Her own back ached as though she had been beaten. Her son worked from dawn until nightfall. And all the while the girl sat humming to herself.

"What a selfish lazybones she is," said the neighbor ants to the Worker's mother, busily carrying away the corn she gave them. "She eats well, doesn't she? Sleeps well, night or day. But lift a finger to help her mother-in-law? Not that one. Oh, no, she's too busy fixing her hair and keeping her hands fine as corn silk. She wants a word or two from someone who knows how to speak out, and a push in the right direction!"

The ants' words only made the Worker's mother resent the girl's idleness all the more. At first she said nothing against her, knowing her son's promise. But goaded by the gossipy ants, she let one word drop, then two, in the girl's hearing. Then came the day when she could bear the sight of her daughter-in-law's idle hands no longer.

"Go on, go on!" the ants whispered at her back. "Speak out!"

But the Worker's mother, her lips white, teeth clenched, eyes glazed with tears of anger, only pushed a grinding stone and pestle in front of the girl. She said no word. Her face said all.

Slowly, the girl knelt behind the grinding stone. She took the heavy pestle in her smooth hands and went gravely to work. But as she worked, she wept. And as she wept, her hands began to bleed. And when her bleeding hands would let her work no more, she waited until the Worker returned from the fields and told him she was going home. He begged her to remain, kissing her fingers, pleading for forgiveness. But she wept and shook her head.

"You promised," she sobbed, "not to make me work. But look at my hands!"

*Sculpture of the Aztec corn goddess*

And he kissed them again, but nothing he could do would persuade her to stay. At midnight she went. No one could stop her. And when she was gone, the Worker and his mother, in all the house, in all the sheds, in all the silos, in all the fields, found only one small ear of corn.